"A DELIGHTFUL STORY YOU'LL NOT WANT TO PUT DOWN UNTIL YOU FINISH IT. YOU WILL TURN EACH PAGE AND WONDER WHAT WILL HAPPEN NEXT. NAOMI MILLER IS A TALENTED AND WONDERFUL AUTHOR, AND I CAN'T WAIT TO READ MORE OF HER STORIES."

~ MOLLY MORRIS JEBBER, AUTHOR OF
TWO SUITORS FOR ANNA

"A DELICIOUS AND DELIGHTFUL STORY WITH A LARGE HELPING OF FUN AND A DASH OF ROMANCE."

~ *JENNIFER BECKSTRAND, AWARD-WINNING AUTHOR OF
THE MATCHMAKERS OF HUCKLEBERRY HILL SERIES*

"I'M READY TO PULL UP A CHAIR IN THE SWEET SHOP, SAVOR A SLICE OF CINNAMON BREAD, AND DIG INTO THIS JUICY MYSTERY."

~ DANA MENTINK – AWARD-WINNING AUTHOR OF THE
LOVE UNLEASHED SERIES

"A SWEET, FUN AND INTRIGUING MYSTERY YOU CAN REALLY SINK YOUR TEETH INTO."

~ RACHEL L MILLER - AUTHOR OF THE AMISH
ROMANCE SERIES: *WINDY GAP WISHES*

LEMON
TART
MYSTERY

BOOKS BY NAOMI MILLER

BLUEBERRY CUPCAKE MYSTERY

CHRISTMAS COOKIE MYSTERY

LEMON TART MYSTERY

PUMPKIN PIE MYSTERY
(Winter 2017)

AMISH SWEET SHOP
MYSTERY

LEMON TART MYSTERY

BY
NAOMI MILLER

PUBLISHING

Lemon Tart Mystery
Copyright © 2017 by Naomi Miller

Lemon Tart Mystery / Naomi Miller

ISBN: 978-0998169217 (Paperback)
ISBN: 978-1386895770 (eBook)
ASIN: B0747BM5GK

1. Fiction / Religion & Spirituality / Christian Books &
Bibles / Christian Fiction. 2. Fiction / Mystery, Thriller &
Suspense / Mystery / Cozy. 3. Fiction / Christian Books
& Bibles / Literature & Fiction / Amish & Mennonite.

2017938039

S&G Publishing, Knoxville, TN
www.sgpublish.com

Cover, graphics and formatting by Expresso Designs

First Edition 2017

To God be the Glory...

GLOSSARY

The German/Dutch dialect spoken by the Amish is not a written language. It is solely dependent on the location and origin of each settlement. The spellings below are approximations.

aenti = aunt
allrecht = all right
appeditlich = delicious
bruder/bruders = brother/brothers
buwe/buwes = boy/boys
danki = thank you
Dat = dad
dochder = daughter
du bischt daheem = you're home
Englischer = non-Amish person
freind/freinden = friend/friends
frau = wife

froh = happy

Gott = God

hochmut = pride

in lieb = in love

jah = yes

kaffe = coffee

kinner = children

kumme = come

maedel/maedels = girl/girls

Mamm = mom

naerfich = nervous

nee = no

onkel = uncle

rumschpringe = running around time for youth

schweschder/schweschders = sister/sisters

verrickt = crazy

wunderbaar = wonderful

A NOTE FROM NAOMI MILLER

Lemon Tart Mystery is one of my favorite stories in this series. I had such fun writing about Mrs. Simpkins and Mr. O'Neal; they are delightful people and lots of fun, too. I hope this story helps you to get a better picture of their lives and how they interact with others in their community.

When I felt the Lord calling me to write Amish fiction that was fun to read, free from stress, anxiety, and other stomach-tightening reactions, I wasn't certain if readers would enjoy it. I'm thrilled to find loyal readers who look forward to the release of new books in the series... many more readers than I expected.

As with any work of fiction, I've taken license in some areas of research as a means of creating circumstances necessary to my characters or plot. I've created fictional characters in a fictional town.

Any inaccuracies in the Amish, Mennonite or English lifestyles portrayed in this book are completely due to fictional license.

God bless you!

~Naomi

A soft answer turneth away wrath:
but grievous words stir up anger.

Proverbs 15:1

For Rachel

ONE

Thursday started out as a normal day for Katie Chupp. As always, she left home just before sunrise, heading toward the small town located not far from her family's farm.

Katie was eager to get to work, where she would create the most delicious breads, cakes, cookies, and assorted pastries that could be found in Abbott Creek.

When she arrived at The Sweet Shop, it

was dark inside. Katie pulled out her key, unlocked the door and stepped inside. After locking the door behind her, she turned on the overhead lights and headed to the kitchen. Comfortable with her daily routine, she went to work, pulling out the ingredients she needed to make nine-grain bread.

Using the large, commercial mixer, she was careful to add everything in the correct order, watching until the dough pulled away from the hooks enough to begin the next step. Then she changed the setting so it would knead the dough until it was ready to knead by hand. She was thankful that the professional mixer did such a *gut* job and that it spared her much time, but the dough still required a human touch to prepare properly.

Sticking to her routine, she knew

precisely what to do. Many mornings found her praying or singing as her hands flattened and pounded dough for one of a dozen breads she baked daily.

Soon she was scraping the dough from the large bowl and working it with her hands on the large countertop. As she squeezed and pressed the dough, flipping the large mound over and repeating her motions again and again, her mind wandered and she thought about how different it was making bread at The Sweet Shop than it was when she baked bread at home.

When making bread for her family, she did every step by hand, mixing and kneading the dough by hand from the very beginning.

Even with so many growing *buwes*, their family rarely used more than ten loaves of bread in any given week. At the bakery, she made two dozen loaves each morning of each type of bread they sold and that was in addition to what had been specially ordered by customers.

Katie carefully separated out bunches of dough, weighing each one before settling them into a loaf pan. After covering the pans with a clean cloth and then setting them aside to let the dough rise, she moved to a nearby counter to mix up the ingredients for snicker-doodles, one of her favorite desserts.

Four dozen cookies were soon baking in the oven, filling the bakery with a delicious, spicy aroma.

Pausing for a moment, she left the kitchen area and made her way to the front of the bakery. The sun was just making an appearance, turning the dark sky to a beautiful pink as it rose slowly toward the sky.

Looking at the clear, blue heavens, Katie could not help thinking that the day might seem a bit too normal. It had been several months since her last adventure—and almost a year since that fateful day when she had arrived at work, only to discover that the bakery had been ransacked.

Many of the breads and pastries, along with some of the customer orders that had already been prepared, had been missing—leaving a huge mess to be dealt with.

But today the sun was rising over the Abbott Creek community, clear and brilliant. Soon the sky would be a beautiful shade of blue. The bakery would open and customers would be arriving to buy delicious, fresh breads and desserts.

Katie would stay in the kitchen most of

the morning—measuring, mixing, shaping, baking and frosting dozens of pastries and cookies. After all the prep work was done, she would start to work on orders taken during the morning.

Katie typically spent her working hours in the kitchen baking delicious treat to keep the bakery cases filled. In between that work, she would work on filling any special orders.

Every day was much the same. Customers came in to order their favorites—or to place special orders. Then those same customers would come back the following day to pick up their orders. And it would start all over again.

Some might think her job boring, but she enjoyed the routine. She knew what to expect each day—and if she wanted variety, there was plenty of that with the orders they received from customers.

Of course, there is also the adventure that comes with each mystery that somehow seems to find me, she thought with some amusement.

Katie was soon back in the kitchen, pulling the snicker-doodles out of the oven.

Dear Gott, danki for giving me such a wunderbaar job. I cannot think of anything I would rather be doing.

A few minutes later, Freida showed up. Freida helped with the baking when Katie had more work than she could manage; otherwise her job was waiting on customers when the bakery opened.

More often than not, she came early to visit with Katie. And she always asked the same thing day after day...

"Don't you ever get tired of doing the same old thing, Katie? Don't you ever wish something different would happen around here?"

Katie laughed before answering her *freind*. "*Nee*. I cannot think of anything I enjoy more than baking."

"And just what is so funny, Katie Chupp?" Freida asked with a hand on one hip and a frown pulling at the corners of her mouth.

"*Ach*, I was thinking just before you arrived how some people might find what we do boring, but there is much about it that changes constantly". Katie pulled another sheet of cookies from the oven before going on.

"Besides, I can remember a morning when something different happened—a morning that was more frightening than anything I have ever known. Even though everything turned out fine, I still remember how scary it was at the time."

"But Katie, it wasn't so bad—not really. And because of it, you met Travis. I think he's a bit *in lieb* with you. It's too bad that's he's an *Englischer*. The two of you make such a cute couple."

"Freida, do not tease me about such a thing. Travis is not *in lieb* with me. We are just *freinden*. That's all."

"You are not fooling me, Katie Chupp. I know what is what. You can deny it all you want, but I know you have feelings for him—and him for you."

"*Ach*, Freida. We cannot—I cannot—have feelings for him. You know this is what has to be. Even if I wanted—"

"Aha! I knew it." Freida was practically

shouting.

"I cannot have feelings for an *Englischer*. I can not. I will not. And that is that. And I do not want to speak of it further."

With that, Katie turned and left the room to return to her baking. No one could have missed the sad expression on her face before she disappeared into the kitchen, especially Freida, who knew Katie so well.

TWO

Freida was forced to wait until there were no more customers waiting to be helped, but as soon as the front of the store cleared, she headed back into the kitchen.

"Katie, please forgive me for upsetting you. You know how *mei* tongue runs away from me at times."

"*Ach*, Freida. Of course I forgive you. I do

think about Travis—more than I should, to be sure. Ever since I painted the windows of the bakery last year, I have been fretting about getting in trouble with the bishop. That is why I cannot make any mistakes, like being more than *freinden* with an *Englischer*."

"But you have not been baptized into the church yet. You are still on your *rumschpringe*."

"That makes no difference, Freida."

"Makes no difference? What if Travis is the one for you?"

"*Nee*, he cannot be the one."

"Why not?"

"Because I would have to leave the church... the community... *mei freinden*... *mei home*."

"*Nee*, you will not be shunned, so long as you do not join the church beforehand."

Freida's voice was full of determination.

"But I would no longer belong. I cannot imagine how horrible that would be."

"Then Travis is not important enough to you; otherwise, you would not hesitate."

Freida sounded sad, which surprised Katie. She wondered how much her freind had thought about leaving her family—and church—behind.

"*Nee*, he is not. I do not know of anyone who is important enough to give up *mei haus* —*mei* faith. Could you leave everything behind for someone, Freida?"

"Truthfully, I do not know, Katie. I only know if you love someone, you should be able to leave everything behind for them."

"And I know that you have been spending time in the romance section of the library again."

Freida blushed before answering back. "It matters not where the knowledge *kummes* from. It does not make it any less true."

"Perhaps not, but life for fictional people is far easier than those of us with flesh and blood."

They were both silent for several minutes while Katie carefully sliced cookies from the long roll of chilled dough.

"In those romance books you fancy, things always work out somehow, typically without anyone having to leave what or who they love behind. It is not that way in real life."

"I know; you are right."

"*Jah*, I am."

Freida grabbed her in a big hug. Evidently she was willing to drop the matter —at least for the time being. "I do not want to lose you as *mei freind*. You are *mei* best *freind*."

"I do not want to lose you as *mei* friend, either. And I do not want to think of leaving *mei* family or *mei* church. *Ach*, why do I have feelings for an *Englischer* when I know it is wrong?"

"Katie, *Gott* will work it out somehow. You have to trust Him. If it is His plan for you and Travis—"

"Please, Freida. Do not say that. I cannot. I cannot even talk of the possibility of a future with Travis. It cannot be."

Both *maedels* turned toward the front room when they heard the tinkle of bells that hung over the bakery's front door.

"We must have a customer. Do you want to go?"

"*Nee,* you go. I have a lot more baking to

do."

"*We* will talk later, *jah*?"

"*Jah*, later."

When Freida left, Katie bowed her head long enough for a quick prayer.

Dear Gott, please show me what to think. Help me to know what to do.

Freida was waiting for Katie after work. It was a beautiful spring afternoon, with the birds singing and a cool breeze blowing through the trees. As they walked home together, Freida chatted about her day.

"Did you see Mrs. Mueller *kumme* in? She always seems to manage to be first. Lately, she sits for a while at one of the tables and watches the other customers coming and going. I think she's a terrible gossip, don't you?"

Without giving Katie a chance to answer, Freida went on. "And not once did Mr. O'Neal come in. He hasn't been by for over a week. He used to come in for cookies several times a week, although I always thought it was an excuse to see Mrs. Simpkins. I thought for sure and for certain that they were dating. Do you think they broke up?"

Katie opened her mouth to answer, but once again Freida went on before she managed to say anything.

"Are you going to the singing? I can sit with you some, but I sort of promised someone else I would spend time with them, too. And I have been thinking about you and Travis. If you truly don't think you could never care enough about Travis to date him, is there a *buwe* in the community that you would be wanting to court?"

"Stop!" Katie laughed. "*Ach*! That is a lot to talk about, Freida. Where do I even begin?"

"*Jah*, well you know how I go on sometimes." Freida looked a bit sheepish, but said nothing else, so Katie took the opportunity to jump in again.

"Well, for one thing, you know I like Mrs. Mueller." Katie sent her *freind* a serious look, but Freida only shrugged and gave a half smile in return.

"I try not to talk about Mrs. Mueller or any of our customers in a hurtful way." Katie paused a moment, before clearing her throat and continuing.

"And as a matter of fact, *jah,* I did notice

that Mr. O'Neal has not been in the bakery for several days. I think the last time I saw him was last Friday. And Mrs. Simpkins hasn't mentioned him to me. She used to sit at the prep table and chat while I worked, but lately she's been staying in her office. I hope nothing has happened between them. They seem perfect for each other."

"That's just what I thought, too. How can we find out if something has happened? And how can we fix it?"

"Look, Freida. I think we need to leave it alone. If something has happened, Mrs. Simpkins and Mr. O'Neal will work it all out."

"*Nee*, Katie. We need to help them."

"Freida, I know how much you want to help," Katie spoke carefully, weighing each word before she replied, doing her best to be tactful. "But I really think it is for the best to stay out of it. Unless Mrs. Simpkins or Mr. O'Neal asks for our help, we should not interfere."

"But Katie—"

"*Nee*, Freida. I will not do anything that might hurt Mrs. Simpkins or Mr. O'Neal. We do not know *Gott's* plans for them, so how can we know the right thing to do?"

"Then I guess we must leave it to *Gott*. You are right, that is the best thing to do. But Katie, you totally ignored *mei* last question. Are you going to the singing? Do you care about Travis, or is there another *buwe* that you want to court?"

"*Jah*, I plan to go to the singing. But *nee*, there is no one I am wanting to court—at least for now. And I am not saying anything more about it, so please don't ask again."

"I guess I have to let it go for now anyway, since I need to get home. But I still think you like Travis..."

And with a smile and a wave, Freida walked away, heading toward her family's farm.

Katie shook her head, let out a sigh, and continued on her way home.

THREE

The next morning, Katie was working on a special order for the Mayor's wife when Freida walked into the kitchen, her eyes sparkling and a wide smile on her face.

Katie was preparing to ask what her *freind* was so excited about—when Mr. O'Neal walked in behind her.

"*Gudemariye*, Mr. O'Neal."

"And a good day to ya, Katie-girl. That's a

fine bit o' work there. You certainly do have a way with the fancy decorating."

Katie ducked her head at the compliment, since it also served as a reminder of the trouble she had almost gotten herself into over decorating the window of The Sweet Shop for Christmas.

"Is Mrs. Simpkins still in her office, Katie?" Freida spoke with such excitement and enthusiasm, Katie wondered what Mr. O'Neal would think.

Katie simply nodded her head, "*Jah*, as far as I know." She knew it would do no good to try to discourage Freida from playing matchmaker with Mr. O'Neal and Mrs. Simpkins.

Even as a young *maedel*, Freida had always been trying to match up her *freinden* and others in the community.

"Did I hear my name, Katie?" Mrs. Simpkins called out as she came around the corner from her office, stopping abruptly before she reached them all. "Oh, hello."

Katie wondered what the reason could be that had turned her employer's voice, normally sweet and friendly, into something strangely unmovable.

"Good morning to ya, Milly. I was wondering if ya would be wanting to take a bite of lunch with me—say around noon?"

Katie heard what sounded like a huff from behind her before Mrs. Simpkins replied, her voice full of ice.

"No, I don't have time for that today." And without another word, she turned and went back into her office.

Mr. O'Neal stood there for several seconds, staring after their boss, his expression changing from cheerful to perplexed as he stared in the direction she had disappeared.

Freida's mouth dropped open and she looked as if she wasn't sure whether to stay— or to run away. Katie was glad her *freind* was standing behind Mr. O'Neal where he couldn't see the surprised look on her face.

She had never known her dear, sweet boss to be so abrupt with anyone—ever. Even when The Sweet Shop was broken into several months ago, Mrs. Simpkins had gone out of her way to help the family involved.

It was a mystery for sure and for certain what Mr. O'Neal, who Katie had thought held a special place in Mrs. Simpkins' heart, could have done to put her in such a mood.

"Well then, I suppose I had better be getting back to the cafe." And without looking at either of them, he turned to leave.

Katie struggled to think of something to say to him, an apology or some sort of explanation about Mrs. Simpkins' odd behavior, but nothing came to mind. A moment later, he was gone.

"What do you think that was all about, Katie?" Freida's voice came out in a harsh whisper and Katie shushed her before answering.

"I have no idea, Freida, but this is not our business and we would do best not to get in the middle of it."

Freida looked at Katie with an expression somewhere between surprise and hurt, but after a few seconds she nodded and turned to go back to the front of the bakery.

Katie stood beside the cake she had been decorating—the icing bag still in her hand—

for all of thirty seconds, before she turned and followed her *freind*.

When she pushed through the swinging doors between the kitchen and the shop, Katie could see that the front room was empty of customers, making it easy to spot Freida, who was busy wiping down a table by the front window.

Katie walked slowly toward the table, speaking softly as she went. "Freida?"

Freida looked up at Katie. Speaking quickly, her words tumbled out in a jumble. "I know I am a gossip. I know I talk too much about things I have no business messing about with. I am sorry, Katie. Please forgive me. I did not mean to stick *mei* nose where it does not belong. You were right to shush me."

The sound of a quiet sniffle reached

Katie's ears before Freida went on.

"For sure and for certain, I only wanted to help."

"Freida, I came out here, not to be forgiving you, but to ask if you can forgive me."

The damp cloth in her hand stilled on the table as Freida looked up at Katie, with a slightly odd expression on her face.

"*Ach,* of course I forgive you, Katie." Freida rushed over to her *freind*, wrapping Katie in a tight hug. "And will you forgive me for being such a busybody?"

"You are not such a busybody, but *jah,* of course I forgive you."

"So what do you think happened between —" Freida quickly covered her mouth with her hand.

"Freida?" Katie prompted.

Looking a bit sheepish, Freida replied. "Never mind, Katie. I think it's time for me to get back to work."

"Are you all right, Uncle?"

Andrew stopped short at the question, looking around the dark cafe until he spotted his nephew seated at a small table in the corner, a thick paperback open in one hand, a cup of tea in the other.

"*Aye*, I am. I'm right as rain, Sean."

The tilt of one eyebrow and ironic twist of his young nephew's lips told Andrew that Sean did not believe him for one second.

"Are you sure of that, Uncle?"

Andrew moved to the table and dropped heavily into the chair across from Sean.

"*Aye,* you're right. I'm not all right and I've not the slightest idea what I can do about it."

"It's that Mrs. Simpkins, isn't it?"

Andrew felt his jaw drop open in shock. It took a moment for him to reply. "What do you know about that?"

"Oh please, Uncle. All anyone has to do to know how you feel about her is to watch the two of you in the same room. A blind man could see it."

"Well, then I wish someone would tell me why she *canna* see it, then."

"I think she does see it. She just doesn't want to admit it." Sean smiled as he sat back.

"You're *thinkin'* she doesn't feel the same, then?"

"I didn't say that. Who knows what

women feel... or want..." Sean stopped talking then and looked back down at his book, though it didn't look to Andrew like he was actually reading the words in front of him.

I wonder what young lass has been giving him a hard time?

He started to ask, but thought better of it. Clearly Sean did not want him to know anything more about it just now.

"What do you think I should do about her?"

Sean looked up, surprise coloring his young features. "If it were me, I would play her own game against her."

Taken aback by the unexpected answer, Andrew waited a moment before asking, "And just how do I go about that?"

"Well, I'll tell you what I would do."

It was hours later when Mrs. Simpkins came back out of her office, walking over to where Katie was putting the finishing touches on the fancy cake.

"By the way Katie, I was wondering... why are there crates of lemons in the pantry? Did we get a large order—or several orders—that we need an abundance of lemons?"

"No, ma'am. Actually I was thinking of trying some new desserts. I thought perhaps it would be a *gut* idea to offer something different for the Memorial Day celebration."

After a moment, Amelia looked back toward the store room, then nodded her head. "All right, dear. I've always trusted your instincts in these matters. You go ahead with your plans. I'm delighted that you're always thinking of ways to keep our customers happy... and maybe draw in some new ones."

Lemon Surprise Cupcakes

Cupcake Ingredients:

1 lemon supreme cake mix

3 large eggs

2 tsp lemon peel, grated

¾ cup water

1/3 cup unsweetened applesauce

1½ cups blueberries, fresh

1 tbsp all-purpose flour

Frosting Ingredients:

3½ cups confectioners' sugar

1-2 tbsp water

1 tsp lemon extract

Instructions:

1. Preheat oven to 350°F.

2. Grease and lightly flour two cupcake pans (making 24 cupcakes. Set aside.

3. Using a mixer on low speed, blend the cake mix, eggs, and water a few minutes until smooth and creamy.

4. Add lemon zest. Stir lightly until combined.

5. Spoon batter evenly into cupcake pans just over halfway.

6. Toss half the blueberries in a tablespoon of flour.

7. Push 3 blueberries into the center of each cupcake.

8. Cover with remaining cake batter.

9. Bake for 15-18 minutes or until a toothpick inserted in the cupcake comes out clean. (Be careful not to insert toothpick into center of cupcake where blueberries are).

10. Remove from the oven and allow to cool before frosting.

LEMON TART MYSTERY

Make the frosting:

1. Using a fork, combine confectioners' sugar, 1 tablespoon water, and lemon extract.

2. Add ½-1 additional tablespoons of water to thin out, if desired.

3. Evenly cover the tops of the cupcakes with frosting.

4. Top each cupcake with 2-3 blueberries

Katie usually makes everything from scratch, but when she discovered Mrs. Simpkins wanted to try making one of her new recipes, she thought it would be best to create a recipe using a store-bought cake mix. Of course, she added a few special touches to it, making it a yummy dessert—one that is often requested and is sure to be a favorite of the Abbott Creek community.

FOUR

Travis drove slowly along the bumpy, unpaved road that led to the Yoder home, thinking of how thankful he was that the close-knit community of plain folks was so giving.

Like most of the other odd jobs he had done over the last few months, he was certain this one was something that any one of a dozen men in the community would normally have pitched in and done for free.

However, because Katie and her mom had made their neighbors aware of his family's needs, her neighbors were constantly asking him to come over and help with this or that—and they always insisted on paying him... and sending food home with him as well.

I owe that girl so much.

He tried to convince himself that his feelings were nothing more than friendship whenever he started thinking about Katie and how much he enjoyed spending time with her.

Oh, who am I kidding? What am I gonna do?

He tried to think about something else... anything else. Fortunately, he spotted the oversized black mailbox that had "Yoder" painted in neat, white block letters beside a long gravel drive and he signaled, slowing down for the turn.

Fences lined either side of the wide driveway. On one side, there were cows grazing; on the other side were horses. He followed the smooth, gravel drive for awhile before a house came into view.

His foot eased off the gas pedal as he pulled into a clearing that stretched out in a wide circle in front of a red barn, a collection of smaller buildings, and a white house with blue shutters. The house stood against the green landscape like something from a postcard or a painting.

There was a peace in the simplicity of the surroundings for as far as he could see; the clear blue sky and thick white clouds were unspoiled by towering wooden poles with miles of wires carrying electricity to houses and businesses.

A knock on his window startled Travis and the car lurched beneath him and stalled when his foot pressed the brake pedal. In his haste he had forgotten the clutch.

He shook his head as the person outside his window started laughing. He didn't even bother to look to see which Yoder it was at his window, especially since the only one he knew by name was Jake. He started the car again, being sure to engage the clutch.

"Yeah... yeah... I'm just a riot." He muttered to himself as he pulled over to the obvious parking area beside the barn.

By the time he had parked and gotten out of the car, three other Yoder boys had joined their brother in the driveway—and two of them were laughing with him.

Jake, however, was not one of the faces

he saw. He came striding out of the barn a minute later, removing a thick pair of work gloves as he walked toward Travis and the other boys.

"Timothy, Levi, I believe you still have stalls to muck out. Thomas, you really ought to get that milk in to *Mamm* right away. And Samuel, those chickens are not going to feed themselves."

Travis watched as the four boys went in different directions, the two younger boys moving a lot quicker than their older brothers.

"Thanks for that."

"Not at all." Jake answered, with only a hint of a smile. "Truth is, they don't see much of that kind of car around here. John Baker drives the twins to their job over at the mill every day, but his vehicle is a truck."

"A truck? I thought he drove a van."

Jake answered, *"Jah,* he drives a van when he is carrying more than two or three passengers."

"So, what is it you need help with, Jake?"

"We need another chicken coop—a really big one. *Mei onkel* and *aenti* are moving to Florida and leaving their chickens with us."

"Another one? But you already have a perfectly good chicken coop. Why would you need another one?" Travis gestured to the little buildings grouped near the barn.

One of those had to be for all those chickens he had driven past a few minutes ago.

"We do, *jah,* but they have over a hundred chickens. There is not enough room in the one we have for that many chickens."

"Oh..." Travis stopped to think about why someone would have that many chickens, but he couldn't come up with any kind of answer that made sense.

"Is it a dumb question to ask why they would have that many chickens?"

Jake laughed before he answered. "No, it is not dumb. They have that many because they sell the eggs. If they sold chickens, they would have several thousand. I am thankful they only sold the eggs."

Well, that makes sense, I guess.

"So, they're leaving them here with your family?"

"*Jah*, because so many people around the area buy the eggs."

"And they're not going to sell eggs in their new community?"

"Actually, they are taking about a dozen

with them. If they have the same kind of demand there as here, they can always buy more chickens."

"Oh, ok. That makes sense."

"*Jah,* I thought so, too."

"Well, but isn't this something you usually make into a group activity... kind of like those barn raisings?"

Jake laughed before he answered. "No, I don't believe we have ever had a chicken coop raising. Guess we could though—if you're too busy."

"No, I'm not too busy." Travis answered quickly. "I just hate to have you pay me for work you could probably have done in an hour or two with some of your neighbors helping you."

"Wait," Jake turned and raised a hand between them. Travis stopped and waited for

Jake to go on. "You were expecting me to pay you?"

To that, Travis had no answer. *Could I have misunderstood?*

He stood there, trying to figure out how to get his foot out of his mouth, when Jake started laughing.

"Travis, I am teasing you."

It took a moment for Jake's words to sink in, but then Travis smiled and pretended to punch Jake on the arm. "Oh yeah, that's a good one, man."

Jake laughed again before turning to walk towards the barn, motioning for Travis to follow him.

Travis followed Jake through the wide double doors and through a large open area that ran the length of the structure. There were stalls lining both sides, but the ones on his right were of various sizes, with different doors and walls.

As they moved through the barn, Travis was surprised at the amount of light inside the enormous building. There were no electric lights that he could see, but there was also no air of gloom that he had expected from a space with no artificial light and only a few windows.

"Should we get started?" Jake stood by a large pile of neatly stacked wood boards.

"Wow. This is going to be quite a chicken coop."

"A hundred chickens." Jake looked over his shoulder at the lumber behind him. "*Jah.*"

He tossed a pair of thick work gloves to Travis and turned to heft several boards onto his shoulder.

Travis pulled the gloves onto his hands

and lifted as much lumber as he could—not quite as much as Jake had, but a respectable amount all the same—and followed Jake back out of the barn.

FIVE

From the middle of the crosswalk, Katie noticed Andrew O'Neal standing outside The Sweet Shop. She watched as he stood there, looking in through the front window. It appeared that he was talking... out loud... but there was no one near him.

She shook her head a little as she continued across the deserted street. For days there had been a thickness in the air between the bakery owner and the cafe owner.

The two of them cannot even be in the same room together. Not that they have been. It is obvious that they are avoiding each other.

The situation was a miserable one. Since the tension had begun, Freida had been plotting how she could get involved, trying to find a way to fix whatever must be wrong between the two *Englischers* she and Katie held most dear.

But nothing she had tried had made any difference. Mrs. Simpkins either disappeared or hid in her office whenever Mr. O'Neal walked into the bakery.

Mr. O'Neal had brought flowers, candy—even the most darling little stuffed elephant for their boss over the last few days, but to no avail.

They most certainly cannot go on this way.

Katie hoped they would find some way to make amends before the festivities of the holiday began. Aside from the delicious treats Katie had been whipping up all week, there was always a wide array of holiday fare that everyone in town enjoyed before the fireworks show began over the lake at sunset.

She had been looking forward to it for weeks. As had everyone else in town.

Katie continued to watch as she finished crossing the street and stepped onto the sidewalk. Mr. O'Neal made no move to go in. He just stood there—talking.

As she slowly approached him, she realized what she had thought was him talking to himself now sounded more like muttering to himself. Besides, there was no one he could possibly be talking to.

Unless he is praying. Englischers pray out loud sometimes.

She knew that to be true because she had heard her *freind* Anna do it on more than one occasion.

With that in mind, Katie prepared to slip past Mr. O'Neal into The Sweet Shop, so that she would not disturb him.

However, when she tried, he stopped her with one word.

"Katie!"

"Oh, hello there, Mr. O'Neal."

He made no effort to move, but he stopped talking. And he continued to look in through the bakery's front window.

"Right. Well, I'll just be getting back to

work now."

"Right!" He answered loudly and shifted his feet a little, but otherwise didn't move or look away from the window.

Katie opened her mouth, closed it a second later, and then spoke again.

"*Jah.*" She stretched the word, more than a little confused by Andrew's odd behavior.

After another few seconds she moved past him and into The Sweet Shop, looking back at him through the window once she was inside.

Walking across the customer area, she looked back several times until she reached the counter... coming upon an equally confused-looking Freida.

"How long has he been standing there like that?"

Freida answered only with a distracted-sounding "Hmm?".

"Freida?"

"*Jah?*" She jumped a little as she said it.

"How long has Mr. O'Neal been standing there like that?"

"He showed up about five minutes after you left for lunch."

"And he has been there the whole time?"

"*Jah,* he has. Only, when he first came, he was pacing back and forth a lot. He would walk to one end of the window and look in. Then he would walk to the other end and look in again. He repeated that about every minute for a long time."

"And he has not *kumme* in?"

"*Nee,* not once."

Katie looked back over at the front window, sparing a glance at all the empty tables between the counter they stood behind and the front door.

"Has anyone *kumme* in while he has been at that?"

"Oh, *jah*. There have been several customers *kumme* in. At least two of them stopped and spoke to him too; one on their way in and one after they left."

"But still he has not *kumme* in?"

"*Nee*. And I could not exactly go out." She turned to look at Katie. "Did you ask him what he is doing?"

"*Nee,* but I did not realize he has been there for *mei* entire lunch break. Do you think I should?"

Freida shrugged, and then said, "Do you think this has something to do with Mrs. Simpkins? They were arguing something fierce the other morning."

"It could be, and if it is, then I certainly

do not want to be involved."

Freida was shaking her head before Katie even finished speaking. "Me either. We have enough to do without getting ourselves involved in a silly argument between two *Englischers*."

Katie answered somewhat distractedly... "*Jah,* you are right," but she continued looking out the front window.

"What is he doing?" Mrs. Simpkins' voice startled both girls.

Katie let out a squeak of surprise and Freida jumped back quickly, a hand to her chest.

"Just how long has he been out there, scaring off my customers?" Mrs. Simpkins' voice was harsher than Katie could ever remember hearing it.

I always thought she liked Mr. O'Neal.

For sure and for certain, it does not sound like that now.

Katie looked over at Freida, who was looking right back at her with a hint of panic in her eyes. Katie shook her head a little, raising her eyebrow at the same time, trying to communicate wordlessly to poor Freida that she hadn't the slightest idea what to do... or say in this situation.

She thought about mentioning to Mrs. Simpkins that she had only just now returned from her lunch break, but since it was her boss who had sent her in the first place, it seemed silly to say anything.

"Well..." Mrs. Simpkins looked from Katie to Freida and back again. "Do you know how long he's been out there—or not?"

When neither *maedel* answered, she spoke again, sounding more and more impatient with each word.

"No? Well, I'll just put a stop to this right now. Excuse me girls." She moved around the two of them, past the end of the counter and then marched through the shop, pushing the front door open... hard.

Neither Katie nor Freida could understand what Mrs. Simpkins or Mr. O'Neal said, but it was obvious to them both that Andrew started out calm enough.

Of course, after Amelia yelled at him for a minute or two, his calm visibly started to fade—and it wasn't long after that the girls could hear both voices raised.

"It's like a train wreck."

Katie looked away from the scene for a moment to peer quizzically at her *freind*. "Whatever do you mean by that, Freida?"

"Isn't that what the *Englischers* say?"

"Yes, I suppose I've heard the *Englischers* say that before, but what does one thing have to do with the other?"

"It's just that this is something you know you shouldn't watch—like a train accident. And it's certainly not something you should enjoy watching, but you just can't seem to tear your attention away."

"Ah, yes. I see what you mean." Katie's voice trailed off as the couple standing outside the front window moved closer together.

Their boss was nearly toe to toe with the cafe owner now and both still looked... and sounded... to be shouting.

"Tis a puzzle indeed what's got into the both of them."

"*Jah.*" Katie answered absently, adding after a moment, "You know I do believe this is the first time I have ever heard Mrs. Simpkins raise her voice for more than a word or two."

"For sure and for certain."

Both girls jumped when Mrs. Simpkins turned unexpectedly, pushing through the front door and moving purposely across the customer area.

Katie made a show of checking the rows of treats in the display case closest to her and Freida grabbed up a damp cloth and started wiping down the long counter in front of her.

Their usually sweet and soft-spoken boss said nothing to either girl as she moved around the front counter area, and then pushed through the swinging doors that led into the kitchen area.

Katie turned to Freida, whose widened

eyes and shocked expression certainly mirrored her own. For a solid minute, neither of them moved, waiting to see if the storm was over—or not.

Just as Katie turned to go into the kitchen, the swinging doors opened and Mrs. Simpkins walked through them again.

"I apologize for that ugly scene, girls. I simply do not know what has gotten into me lately."

Katie started to speak, but Mrs. Simpkins held up a hand to stop her.

"I know I can trust you girls not to spread rumors all over town, but I'm certain some of our neighbors will not be quite so close-lipped." She took a deep breath before going on... and that was when Katie realized that there was a purse strap over her shoulder.

"I am going to go home and relax. Why don't you girls lock up a bit early and go on home as well. I'll pay you for the rest of the day. I'm just not certain if you want to hang about and deal with the gossips."

"You two can go on home if you want, but I think I had better stay. Travis is coming by in about three hours to pick up the Mayor's cake."

"Oh, I had forgotten completely about that."

Freida spoke up then. "I can stay, too. No one is expecting me home anytime soon—and this way we can just stay open."

"*Jah,* and mayhaps we can head off some of the gossip while we are at it."

"That is very kind of you girls, but you don't have to worry about that." She stopped talking, and looked around the shop absently for a moment before going on.

"Three hours from now is still a bit early. Just you go ahead and close up when Travis gets here. That way you both still get a bit of a break."

"*Jah*, we'll do just that." Katie answered quickly, trying to put her boss's mind at ease.

Travis walked in the front door a full twenty minutes before Katie expected him and he wasted no time in asking Katie about the afternoon. "Is it true what I'm hearing all over town—that Mrs. Simpkins and Mr. O'Neal got into a fight right out front?"

Katie immediately shushed him and turned, going back into the kitchen *by way of* the swinging doors. Travis followed a moment later, curiosity on his handsome features.

"Has Mrs. Simpkins left for the day?"

"*Jah*, she left earlier than usual today— and she told us to close the bakery after you came by to pick up the Mayor's cake."

"Is it safe to talk, then? Come on, Katie, you have to tell me what's going on." Travis looked as puzzled as Katie felt.

"I don't really know anything, except that Mr. O'Neal had been standing around outside the bakery and when Mrs. Simpkins noticed him, she went out and after a few minutes, they began shouting at one another." Katie looked a bit uneasy talking about it.

"When he left, Mrs. Simpkins came back inside, but she didn't say anything about it, except to apologize for the disruption and to say she was going home early."

"Oh, man. That doesn't sound good. I was sure they were dating—or in some sort of relationship. It sounds like they've broken up now, doesn't it?"

"Travis, do you think it could be that serious? Katie was close to tears. "Anyone could see that Mr. O'Neal has been trying to court Mrs. Simpkins for some time. I cannot think what could have happened to upset her so."

She looked up at Travis, waiting for him to speak. He stepped closer before answering, putting a hand on each of her shoulders and squeezing gently.

"I haven't heard anything from any of our customers when I've made deliveries. I had no idea anything was wrong—until this afternoon."

Then he pulled her close for a hug. "Don't worry, Katie. I'm sure they'll work it out. They're perfect for each other."

Much too soon—and with more than a little reluctance—Katie forced herself to pull away. After quickly swiping at her eyes, she smiled at him.

"I am certain you are right. And now you must get going. You do not want to be late delivering the Mayor's cake."

"Right. Well, then I guess I'll see you later."

After Travis left, Katie and Freida turned off the lights and locked the door, before heading to their homes.

SIX

Monday morning, Katie hesitated as she reached to unlock the door of The Sweet Shop. She looked around, taking in the scenery around her.

Nothing was amiss... and she didn't expect to find anything. But for the past few days, she had felt out of sorts, even nervous, when she reached the bakery.

The first time it had happened, she wasn't sure what to think, especially when she stepped inside the bakery and found nothing out of place. It had looked just the same as it had when she left it the day before.

Katie hadn't mentioned it to anyone. Then it had happened again the next morning... and the next... and again today.

What is happening to me? Could this have anything to do with what happened last July?

Though everything had worked out the previous July, when there had been a break-in at the bakery. Katie had been the first to discover the disaster that had been left behind by the young thieves. Freida, one of her co-workers, had arrived moments later to find the door locked—and Katie standing just inside the doorway, looking around at the mess.

The girls had run across the street to The Coffee Cup, where Katie had called Mrs. Simpkins, the owner of the bakery. Then she and Freida had waited for Mrs. Simpkins to arrive with a police officer.

Could I still be worrying over that?

Katie thought over it while she went about her usual morning routine.

Finding the mess, not knowing what had happened, or if there was someone still inside the bakery who might have harmed her or Freida, had been a difficult enough thing that day, but the rushing around for that entire day trying to bake replacements for everything that had been destroyed or stolen was what Katie remembered most.

Nee, that was almost a year ago. I've hardly ever thought of it. Besides which, it all turned out to be a gut thing.

While out making deliveries, Katie had inadvertently discovered a clue to the mystery and the reason behind it. Soon the entire community had become involved in helping a family in need.

Katie had become *freinden* with the children in the Davis family, especially Travis, Gwen, and young Bobby. Travis still worked part-time at the bakery, and Mrs. Simpkins had told Gwen there would be a place there for her soon.

And Mrs. Davis is recovering nicely and able to do more around the house, making it possible for Gwen to work outside the home. Which is a very *gut* thing indeed.

Dear Gott, I don't know what is causing me to be naerfich about this now. Why do I worry that something bad will happen? I am ashamed that I did not ask for help the first time I felt this way. I know you have control over all. I ask you to please take this from me. Help me to put mei trust in you and to not be afraid for nothing. Help me to find mei joy again. In Jesus' name. Amen.

An hour or so later, Katie looked up from her mixing at the sound of the back door opening. She was surprised to see her boss arriving so early, but she was especially surprised—and curious—at the sour expression on Amelia Simpkins' usually sweet features.

"Good morning."

The curt response was so very unlike her normally chatty boss, Katie could not help but worry... and wonder at what was really going on with her, but she schooled her features to be pleasant, making certain there was nothing her boss could find objectionable.

"*Gudemariye*, Mrs. Simpkins. How are you this fine morning?" Katie waited, but no reply came. Mrs. Simpkins went directly into her office without another word.

Katie went back to work, sending up a silent prayer that whatever was bothering her *wunderbaar* employer, *Gott* would help her through it.

After several minutes, Katie went back to humming quietly while she worked. Once a dozen loaves of bread were baking, she mixed the batter for peanut butter cookies, enjoying the delicious aromas floating around the kitchen.

Freida walked in a few minutes before her shift was to start.

"*Gudemariye,* Katie."

"*Gudemariye,* Freida. How are you this morning?" Katie looked up at her *freind,* but did not stop stirring the batter she was preparing.

"I am *gut.* And you?"

"*Gut, jah.*" Katie answered, then she motioned silently to the office where their boss had been since she arrived, widening her eyes in an attempt to let Freida know that something odd was going on.

When Freida looked questioningly at Katie, she mouthed the word "later" to her *freind.* Fortunately, Freida picked up on

Katie's meaning right away. Otherwise, she might have asked something about the fight they had both witnessed the day before and Katie was not at all certain how Mrs. Simpkins—if she heard them talking—would take such a thing.

Freida nodded and went about the business of opening up. The next thirty minutes were busy ones while she helped to fill the shelves with fresh breads and desserts that Katie had been baking this morning for customers.

Then she wiped down the tables and made certain everything was ready for customers before unlocking the front door and turning the sign around to show that the bakery was open and ready for business.

Five minutes before the bakery opened, Mrs. Simpkins walked out of the office. She looked much more her usual self, smiling widely, eyes bright and full of excitement.

"You know, that internet is really something. Katie, have you used the internet much?"

Surprised by the sudden change, more than the actual question, Katie could only shake her head.

To which Mrs. Simpkins waved a hand in dismissal. "Silly question. Sorry. Where is my head today?" She turned to go back into her office, but whirled back to face Katie, adding. "You know, you are on that running around time now, right?"

Katie nodded her head, uncertain where her boss was going with her question.

"Then you could use it without getting in

trouble. And you're welcome to use the computer here anytime you need to—or if you just want to."

"So, what about the internet has you so excited, Mrs. Simpkins?"

At the sound of her voice, they both looked over at Freida. Katie hadn't heard her *freind* push through the kitchen doors, but evidently she had heard enough of the conversation to be curious.

Not that it takes much to pique Freida's curiosity.

"I found the most wonderful site this morning. Those search engines really are helpful, aren't they?"

Freida started to speak, but stopped herself and nodded her head a little instead, which set Katie's own curiosity humming.

What does Freida know about the

internet? Who would have showed her? And just when would she have found the time?

"Katie, are you listening?"

Katie shook her head and turned her attention back to Freida and Mrs. Simpkins. "*Nee,* I am sorry. *Mei* mind wandered for a moment. What did you say?"

"Mrs. Simpkins was just saying that she hopes we can take care of things here for three weeks without her."

Katie looked from Freida... to Mrs. Simpkins... and back to Freida. The wide eyes and shocked expression on her *freind* told her she had missed something big.

"And why would we be taking care of things here by ourselves for three weeks?"

"Because I am going on a cruise!" The words came out in a half squeal and Katie realized it was the most excited she had seen her boss in quite some time.

"A cruise—isn't that exciting, Katie?"

"I'm guessing that is the website you found this morning that has you so excited."

"Yes, it is. I have always wanted to go on a cruise, but my dear Henry suffered from the worst seasickness, it felt cruel to even suggest such a thing."

Mrs. Simpkins' expression dimmed for a moment before she went on, "I know I could have gone years ago, but I didn't think of it at first. Then later, when I thought about going, I had the bakery to think of."

"And now? You still have the bakery."

Katie wanted to shush Freida, but at the same time she wanted to hear the answer, so she said nothing.

"I know I do, but you girls handle most everything. Katie does the baking. You take care of the customers. I don't even place the orders. I just write checks and answer the phone now and then."

Katie started to speak, but Mrs. Simpkins held up a hand to stop her.

"Now, now. I am not bothered by any of that. I like having you girls here. Truth be told, I don't know what I would do without the two of you. You keep this place going. That is why I figure you can handle a few weeks without me. And a trip in the fall, after the summer business has quieted down, but before Thanksgiving, seems like the perfect time."

"It sounds like a wonderful idea to me."

Katie looked over at Freida, surprised to hear such support where there had been panic only moments ago.

"I think so, too." Mrs. Simpkins looked at

both girls, before going on. "So, you'll be all right for three weeks without me?"

"Why three weeks? How long does a cruise take? I guess I was thinking a cruise wouldn't last more than a week."

"Well, it's actually a ten day cruise, but it leaves from New York. I've never been there and thought it would be a good idea to have some extra time to spend in the city."

"That sounds like a very *gut* idea... doesn't it Katie?"

"It does, for sure and for certain." Katie answered quietly. " I have not been to New York in years. For sure, we only drove through the City and made only a few stops. *Mei* cousin Leah lives upstate in a small community."

Thinking of her sweet, sad cousin reminded Katie that it had been some time since she had written a letter. She made a mental note to write to Leah when she arrived home that evening.

"I didn't know you had family there, Katie. I would be tempted to ask you to come with me..." Mrs. Simpkins trailed off a bit and Katie could see where her thoughts were headed, but she would need them both to stay and keep the bakery going in her absence.

"*Nee*, you need us here. Besides which, you should have time to enjoy yourself without worrying over the bakery."

"You're right about that." She started to turn, but stopped and looked at Katie and then Freida in turn. "So, this is okay with the two of you then?"

Freida spoke up first. "Of course it is; it's fine with us. We want you to go and have a *gut* time—and tell us all about it when you get back."

"*Jah,* for sure and for certain we will want to hear all about it." Katie wanted to add something about taking lots of pictures... she did like to look at pictures of exciting places, but she did not want to bring any more trouble down on her head with the church leaders, so she kept quiet.

Fortunately, Mrs. Simpkins solved the problem for her. "I'll be sure to take lots of photos, too. I will take so many pictures, you'll both feel like you were right there with me."

Katie smiled, then laughed a little as Freida practically threw herself at Mrs. Simpkins, wrapping her arms around her in a tight hug.

"Oh, *danki,* Mrs. Simpkins. Really, that

would be *wunderbaar gut!*"

"Excellent. Well, now that it's all settled, I'll just go make some more plans. There is so much to see in the city. I don't want to miss anything important." With that, she turned and went back into her office. Katie and Freida looked at each other with nearly identical grins.

"Do you think she is going just to get away from you know who?" Freida whispered loudly as she made a show of motioning toward the front of the bakery.

Katie didn't even have to wonder who her *freind* meant. "I am thinking that is a part of it, but why would she wait so long if that were all there is to it?"

"*Gut* point." Freida chewed at her lower lip for a moment until the bell over the front door announced a customer. Quickly she rushed through the double doors to the front room.

After she was gone, Katie thought over the conversation and the timing again.

It cannot be that she would do such a drastic thing—just to get away from Mr. O'Neal. She said she has always wanted to take a cruise. I am certain that is all there is to it. But then, what is going on between her and Mr. O'Neal?

Dear Gott, why does she get so upset with him? What could have happened between them? Please help them to work out their troubles. If they cannot be a couple, please help them to be freinden again, if it be your will.

Katie's Triple Lemon Cookies

Cookie Ingredients:

1 cup butter

1 cup white sugar

2 eggs

2 tsp lemon peel, grated

1 tbsp evaporated milk

2½-3 cups self-rising flour

½ cup sour lemon drops, crushed

Frosting Ingredients:

1 cup confectioner's sugar

1 tsp lemon flavoring

1 tsp water

Instructions:

1. Cream the butter and sugar together.

2.   Add beaten egg, evaporated milk, and lemon peel.

2.   Combine the flour and crushed lemon drops; mix with other ingredients.

3.   Spread on a greased baking sheet.

4.   Bake at 350°F for 20 minutes.

4.   Cool before removing to wire rack.

SEVEN

Travis reached up to wipe the sweat out of his eyes. For three days he and Jake had been working on the chicken coop—what seemed like an enormous chicken coop. Even after three days, it felt like they might never finish it.

"Travis, you won't believe it. Levi let me drive their pony cart! It was great!"

Just in time, Travis caught the bullet that

was his youngest brother, looking at his flushed face and laughing at the excitement in his voice over something so seemingly small.

"Looks like you had fun."

"I did! I really did. It was great. Levi was really nice, too. I've had so much fun. Can I come with you tomorrow? Levi said I was welcome anytime. So can I, please? Can I?"

Knowing Bobby well, Travis waited for the questions to slow down. Once he got wound up about something, a person just had to wait for him to get it all out.

"Whoa there. Slow down, buddy. I don't know if you can come tomorrow yet or not. We need to ask mom about that."

Bobby didn't argue or fuss, something Travis really loved about his sweet, precocious baby brother—and something he wished his other brothers would pick up on. He just grinned and hugged Travis.

"So, can I go help Levi in the barn until you're done?"

Travis looked over toward the barn for Jake's younger brother, and sure enough, he stood just outside the barn doors watching them, bucket in hand.

"I guess it's okay. Just don't be in the way, buddy."

"I won't. I promise!" And just like that, Bobby was twisting out of his brother's arms and racing across the yard.

Travis watched until Bobby reached Levi —as he took Bobby's hand and led him around the side of the barn—before he went back to work, sending the nail home that he had already set in place.

"He's really *gut* with the little ones. He

will be a great *dat* some day." Jake's voice took Travis by surprise, but it was his words that really got his attention.

"He can't be more that fifteen. You really start thinking about that kind of stuff so early?"

Jake looked at him with an odd expression. "Why shouldn't he?" When Travis said nothing, Jake went on. "Do you mean to tell me you never think about meeting a nice *maedel*... a nice girl... and settling down, having a family of your own?"

Travis started to laugh until he looked at his friend and realized that Jake was serious.

"You're serious?"

"*Jah*, we take family very serious." He laughed as he gestured toward the field, where several of his brothers were working. "Don't try to tell me you have never noticed."

"Yeah, well..." Travis trailed off as he joined Jake in laughing.

"It's one thing to have a big family..." Travis laughed again when he realized that almost every Amish family he had worked with over the last few months had between four and ten children. "... and quite another to start thinking seriously about having a family at our age."

"I started thinking about having a family at Levi's age." After a moment, Jake added, "Well, maybe a bit older."

Travis stood there a moment, looking at his friend—who he was pretty sure was the same age as he—and started to see just how different the two of them were.

And then, completely unbidden, an image of little Katie Chupp floated into his mind and he found himself thinking about

Christmas—when he had held the ladder for her while she'd painted the front window of the bakery.

He thought about the times she had sat quietly in the passenger seat of his car as he sped along in the early morning, taking her to work.

Then he thought about her standing on his front porch with her mom, holding an enormous basket full of food and treats—and a real Amish quilt for his mother, who had always wanted one, but had never been able to afford to buy one.

He thought about all the times he teased her when he came to pick up the morning deliveries at the back door of the bakery, about her sweet, shy smile and her big, expressive eyes—and he realized maybe Jake wasn't so different after all.

"You know, you should *kumme* to one of our singings." Jake's voice interrupted his thoughts—and Travis was surprised at how much he wanted to snap at his friend for it. Instead, he forced his voice to be calm as he turned his attention back to the board in front of him.

"Is that even allowed?"

"*Jah,* we have visitors at the singings a lot. It's the church services we are hesitant about—though that is mostly because they are in *Dietsch.*"

"Yeah, I don't think I would enjoy sitting through a church service if I can't understand a word of what anyone is saying."

Jake smiled before he answered. "You never know. You might start to pick it up."

He has a point.

Travis thought about all the words Jake used in their conversations that used to sound so foreign to him. Jake tried at times to use the English word as an explanation, but he didn't always remember. It came as a surprise to Travis to realize that he understood quite a few of the *Dietsch* words.

"So, how often do you have these singings?" Travis worked to keep his voice nonchalant, but inside he was wondering how he could ask if Katie came to the singings without raising Jake's suspicions.

Fortunately, he didn't have to worry about figuring it out.

"We are having one here at our *haus* tonight. You should *kumme*. Katie and Freida are bringing cookies."

Travis smiled as he swung the hammer. "I just might do that."

"I know you eat the cookies that Katie bakes. You probably get to sample her baking every day! Anyway I heard she is bringing some lemon cookies—a new recipe she just made up. You don't want to miss those. We get to be her penny pigs."

"Wait! What? By any chance do you mean guinea pigs?"

"*Jah*, that's it—I think. If that means we get to sample her new cookies."

Travis laughed and nodded. Then, because he couldn't pass up the opportunity to tease his friend, he added, "Yeah, that's a tough job."

"Somebody has got to do it." Jake laughed —even as he answered. "Seriously, Travis, you should *kumme*."

"Okay, I will. What time does it start?"

"The youth start arriving at six. Of

course, you will want to go home and clean up when we are done here."

"Yeah, definitely. When should I be here?"

"Anytime after five. I should be done with chores by then." Jake smiled as he answered.

"Great, I'll see you then."

"Katie, did you hear about the cafe?" Hannah was nearly as loud as the bells over the door as she rushed into the bakery that afternoon.

Katie waited until her *freind* had *kumme* to a stop beside the front counter before she answered. "*Nee,* I didn't."

"Ada Mueller stopped in for lunch and

there were rodents inside."

"Wait, what?" Katie shook her head as Hannah's words truly began to sink in. "Oh no! Why would there be rodents in the cafe?"

"I don't know."

"Was Mr. O'Neal there?"

"*Jah,* he was there. She said he was trying to set a trap for them."

"What else did she say?" Katie was leaning across the counter now, eager for more of the intriguing story.

"She said..." Hannah stopped mid-sentence—and it took no more than a moment for Katie to figure out why.

Mrs. Simpkins stepped up to the counter beside Katie.

"Hello, Hannah. How are you today?"

Hannah smiled sweetly. "I am *wunderbaar gut,* Mrs. Simpkins. How are you?"

"I am just fine, dear."

Hannah said nothing else, but waited there, nervously looking from Katie to Mrs. Simpkins, and back to Katie, as Mrs. Simpkins busied herself with the cash drawer from the register.

Katie made a show of arranging the muffins she had brought out just before Hannah had burst through the door. Hannah stepped over to the large display case and pretended she was looking over the selection.

"Have you made a decision yet, Hannah?"

Katie nearly yelped in surprise at the nearness of Mrs. Simpkin's voice. Fortunately, Hannah chose that moment to answer Mrs. Simpkins, covering any noise that might have escaped Katie.

"No ma'am, I haven't. Not yet."

"All right, then. Well, I'm certain Katie can take care of you from here." She turned toward the swinging doors, tossing one last comment over her shoulder as she moved through them. "You can go back to gossiping about the cafe now."

When the kitchen doors closed, Katie and Hannah looked at each other for a full ten seconds before they burst into laughter.

EIGHT

Katie looked around for Freida when she walked into the crowded barn. She did not see her *freind*, but she did see a lot of young people she had never met before at the singing tonight.

She had a moment to think how glad she was that she had made a double batch of cookies to bring tonight since there was quite a crowd around her. *Thanks at least in part to the generous space in the Yoder's barn, for sure and for certain.*

After dropping off her cookies on one of the tables piled high with snacks and deserts, she wandered over to where one of the Yoder *buwes* stood stirring an enormous pitcher of lemonade.

"Hullo Katie Chupp. How are you this fine evening?" Levi Yoder stood beside his *bruder*, handing out plastic cups of lemonade.

"I am *wunderbaar gut* Levi... and you?"

"I'm great. Excited to be here."

She turned to his younger *bruder* then. "And young Samuel—how are you this evening?"

There was an excitement in his eyes that she recognized from her own initial singings.

She had plagued her own *bruder* with questions for months before their parents had finally decided she was old enough to go and see for herself.

"I am *gut,* Katie." He leaned closer when she stepped toward him to make room for others who stepped up behind them for lemonade. "This is *mei* first singing."

His wide eyes had told her that, but she returned his whisper, as if the two of them shared some delicious secret.

"Exciting, isn't it?"

"*Jah,* it most certainly is that."

As more young people crowded around the table, Katie moved away. "Have fun tonight, young Samuel."

"I'll see you later then, Katie?"

"*Jah,* I will be around." And with that, she stepped away from the table, taking the first sip of her lemonade.

It took no more than that sip for her to know that Mary Zook had made it. Her lemonade had been well-known as the best in the district for as long as Katie could remember.

Katie made her way around the edges of the barn, watching for Freida, nodding her head across the crowded room to a few other *freinden—and smiling as she caught small snatches of conversations.*

Quite a few of the young people were talking about the ruckus that happened this afternoon at Mr. O'Neal's cafe. Several people stopped her as she went by them to ask if she knew more about the situation, to which she replied honestly that she knew even less than the others.

Anna Miller was one of the *freinden* who

stopped Katie to ask about it. When she discovered Katie did not know about the latest news, she pulled Katie aside.

"Katie, *kumme* outside with me for a moment?"

Katie followed, smiling to herself. That was one of the things she liked most about Anna. Even though she lived just on the edge of town—and caught sight of the goings on that no one else knew about, she was not a gossip.

Anna waited until they had moved through the side door of the barn before she turned to face Katie.

"Katie, I am worried over this thing at the cafe that everyone is talking about. I do not know how, but I believe Mr. O'Neal's nephew must be involved somehow, and perhaps—," she looked over both shoulders quickly before leaning closer to Katie, "... he has done something illegal."

Katie covered her mouth to smother the gasp that escaped her lips.

"Something... illegal?" Katie breathed the words, shocked at the very idea.

"*Jah,* that is what has me worried." Anna answered, obviously concerned.

Katie watched as she twisted a paper napkin between her hands, pulling it tighter with each motion.

"What makes you think so?" Katie tried to tell herself there was no evidence of such a thing... merely what Mrs. Mueller had been telling people in town.

"There were police at the cafe when I left to *kumme* to the singing."

That got Katie's attention. Police most certainly could mean something illegal had taken place.

"What makes you think Mr. O'Neal's nephew is involved?"

"That part I heard from Mrs. Mueller. She stopped by to talk to *Mamm* this afternoon. We were in the front hallway cleaning when Mrs. Mueller knocked at the door." Her fingers gripped the napkin even tighter and Katie watched as several tiny bits fell off the tattered paper.

"I did not mean to listen, but you know how she talks so loudly when she is excited about something. It is difficult not to hear her."

Katie nodded. "*Jah,* you are right about that."

"What can we possibly do to help Mr. O'Neal? He is such a nice man—and his cafe is just *wunderbaar*. We eat there several times a week, you know."

Katie nodded again. "I eat there often, too. His food is *wunderbaar gut.*" Most everyone in town did the same... and for the very same reason. "I think all we can do is pray and leave the rest up to *Gott,* Anna."

"*Jah*, I know you are right, Katie. That is why I wanted to talk to you about this."

"And perhaps we should keep this to ourselves." Katie kept her voice low.

"*Jah,* for sure and for certain. Everyone else seems to have plenty of gossip to spread already."

At that, Katie giggled. "*Jah,* sure enough."

Laughing, the two girls linked arms and made their way back to the barn.

Barely had Katie walked in the door when Freida appeared out of nowhere, pulling Katie away from Anna. Katie began to object, but Anna appeared relieved to remove herself from the goings on so Katie followed Freida willingly.

"Katie, where have you been?"

Katie started to answer, but Freida rushed on.

"I have been looking for you all over. I am sorry to be so late, but David took forever with his chores this afternoon. I thought he would never be ready to go."

Again, Katie started to speak, but Freida interrupted. "How long have you been here? Did you bring the cookies?

"*Jah*, I—" She began, but did not get to finish her answer.

"*Gut*. I am starving. Let's go get some." And then Freida was pulling Katie over to the refreshment tables.

Singing Night Lemonade

Ingredients:

    1½ cups fresh lemon juice (7 large lemons)

    6 cups water

    ¾ cup sugar (or to taste)

    2 tbsp honey (raw works best)

Instructions:

1. Squeeze lemons or use a juicer until you have 1½ cups of juice.
2. Dissolve sugar in water, stir well.
3. Add honey and stir.
4. Add lemon juice to the mixture.
5. Stir together until well-mixed.
6. Serve chilled or over ice.
7. Sing the night away.
8. Refrigerate leftovers *(if there are any)*.

Important note: this recipe has been adapted for a 2 quart yield. The amount of lemonade needed for the typical Amish youth singing would be at least ten times the amounts listed above.

──────NINE──────

Travis watched Katie from across the barn for a long time. While he watched, he thought about what Jake had said earlier about family.

Why, when I look at Katie Chupp, does the idea of having a family of my own sound really appealing?

After what Amber said, he had decided to

swear off romance—and he had not given serious thought to any certain girl in the two years since—at least not until Jake had mentioned family... and Katie had come to mind.

And why am I thinking of her that way? I can't date her. I can't marry her. I'm certainly not keen on the idea of becoming Amish for her.

And, as uninterested as he was in changing his whole life for a girl, he would never consider asking her to give up her own beliefs for him.

So what am I doing? Why am I still even thinking about this?

He purposely took his attention off Katie and looked around the large, open room, spotting several girls he recognized from town.

It was nearly another minute before he moved over to the refreshment table and picked up two large cups of lemonade. Glancing around, he slowly made his way to the small group of girls.

He had not taken more than three steps before one of the girls looked right at him, blushed to the tips of her ears, then turned and rushed away.

He watched as she went, wondering what her quick exit was all about... and trying to figure out why she looked so familiar, yet he couldn't quite place her.

Before he reached the group of girls, someone pulled at his arm a little and he turned to see who it was.

"You should catch her before she goes too far. The Yoder farm is large and she could get lost easily."

The young woman looked familiar to him as well, but he couldn't think of her name or where he'd seen her—and before he could ask she was gone.

He turned to search the crowd for her and spotted the other girl rushing off toward the dark fields.

Muttering under his breath, he set down the two cups of lemonade and rushed off after her. She would certainly get lost in the dark fields.

They were halfway across the nearest field when he caught up to her, calling out as he reached for her shoulder.

"Hey, come back to the singing. I didn't mean to startle you."

She stopped, but didn't turn so he tried again.

"Is there something wrong? Are you

okay?"

The only response he saw was a shake of her head—which told him nothing really. Was she saying she was not okay or was she saying there was nothing wrong?

What do I do? He waited for nearly a minute before speaking again.

"If there's something going on, you can tell me. Maybe I can help."

She turned then—and something about her face caught his attention.

"I can explain..." Her voice clicked something into place and he was shocked when he recognized her.

"What are you doing here? And dressed like..." He waved a hand at the outfit he was certain must belong to one of the older girls she had been standing with. "... like that!"

Even though he had seen much trashier

clothing in the city, there was no doubt in his mind that she was trying to look like a young woman of eighteen or older. Her clothing was just demure enough that she would not offend the Amish teens, while still loudly proclaiming her an adult.

"There is nothing wrong with what I am wearing."

"Except that it makes you look about five years older."

"And that's a bad thing, why?"

"Because you're fourteen, that's why."

With that, she wilted. The defiance melted from her features. Her shoulders dropped in a slump. And he was certain he saw tears shining at the corners of her eyes.

Travis pulled his sister close, hugging her tightly, ashamed at the vehemence of his outburst as she sobbed hopelessly against his chest.

"I just wanted to... to..."

She never finished, but Travis felt certain he knew what she was getting at. She might only be fourteen, but she was obviously not a little girl anymore.

"Listen, why don't I take you home?"

She looked up then with such panic in her eyes that Travis felt his heart plummet. All he had been trying to do was the right thing —while getting his baby sister away from the much older guys—but somehow it felt like he had done the wrong thing.

"Do we have to tell mom about this?"

He exhaled deeply in relief. He hadn't been so wrong after all.

"No, we don't have to tell mom about this."

As soon as the words were out of his

mouth, he worried he should maybe take them back. Shouldn't their mother know what her fourteen year-old daughter was up to—coming out here late at night... and dressed this way?

Looking at Gwen's worried, tear-stained eyes, he could see that while their mom should certainly know what her daughter was up to, perhaps now was not the time to rat out his baby sister.

"Are you sure you're not going to tell her? You look like you're rethinking what you just said."

"I am, but that doesn't mean I'm a rat. I don't have to tell mom as long as you promise this is the last time you do something like this."

She didn't say anything... just watched him with those big eyes.

"Deal?"

Finally, when he was certain he would have to throw her over his shoulder to get her out of here, she answered, shoulders slumping again.

"Deal."

"Good. okay then, let's get you home."

He took her hand as they moved through the field, wanting to be certain he didn't lose her in the dark.

As they moved back toward the brightly lit barn, his thoughts strayed again to Katie. She was in there somewhere.

Stop that.

He was determined to get his mind off the young woman whom he had no right thinking of in that way... or any way other than as a friend, for that matter.

The thoughts and emotions that were

struggling for attention within him were confusing at best, and terrifying at worst.

Why did Jake have to get started on family today? Nothing of the kind had crossed his mind in more than a year.

I don't have time for this nonsense right now. He shook his head, trying to dislodge the unwelcome thoughts.

Mom is finally getting better. That alone was a great comfort to him right now. Not to mention, he was finally getting his family back on their feet.

And the boys are behaving. That thought reminded him of his young sister whom he was still holding tight to—who seemed determined to grow up too fast.

Just like Jake and his brothers.

It was too ridiculous for words. Who on earth started thinking about getting married and having a family at fourteen?

One look at his baby sister was all it took to tell him she had certainly been thinking about it. It was obvious in everything from the make-up on her face to the set of her jaw.

It was also clear she had been doing more than just thinking—the outfit proved that. She had not just found those clothes lying around in her room.

She's planned for this. The thought made Travis wonder if this was the first time she had been to one of these singings—or even if she had snuck off to the city with her older friends.

Rubbing a hand over the sudden pain across his brow, he didn't notice Katie walking up to them.

TEN

Katie watched as Travis pulled his sister through the field and across the large, open area where buggies and a few cars were parked.

Neither of them looked particularly happy. It wasn't too difficult to figure out why. For sure and for certain, she would not be happy to find one of her own *schweschders* in such attire.

When Travis stopped and rubbed a hand over his forehead, concern filled Katie and she found herself moving toward them.

"Katie." Gwen was the first to notice her. A deep, red stain spread across her cheeks and up to the tips of her uncovered ears as she spoke.

Travis looked up sharply at his sister's words. His expression darkened when he spotted Katie walking toward them.

Conflicting emotions rushed through her. There was hurt. There was confusion. There was even curiosity—at what she could possibly have done to warrant such anger...

She tried to tell herself that she was being silly. There was no reason to believe that his expression had anything to do with her appearance.

Perhaps he is angry that I have seen Gwen

dressed up in such a manner.

Calm flowed over the confusion and hurt.

Of course! That has to be it. He is upset over me seeing his baby schweschder looking this way.

Thinking of it that way, now Katie was unsure whether she should stay—or go. Clearly they were not in need of any help and neither seemed very happy to see her.

But as she turned to go, Gwen spoke up.

"Katie, are you leaving? We could give you a ride home."

She started to answer, but Travis jumped in, beating her to it.

"Nonsense, Gwen. Katie just got here. She wouldn't want to leave so soon."

Something about his answer made Katie want to argue—just to catch him off guard. She might have pushed the urge away if it was not for the expression on his face.

He looks like he is just so certain of himself... that, of course, he is right.

"Actually, it would be *wunderbaar* if you could give me a ride home. Freida will not want to leave for some time and I am tired. It is so *gut* of you to offer me a ride."

She hid a grin when Travis snapped his mouth shut.

"Great." Gwen answered, sounding considerably more cheerful than she had a moment before. "You can even sit up front."

Travis turned and walked in the direction of his car, muttering something under his breath as he went. Katie nearly laughed at the absurdity of it all.

Something is bothering him—something other than his schweschder. I wonder what it could be.

Katie slid into the older vehicle. She was familiar with the car by now, having ridden in it on many occasions. After pulling the door shut, she turned in her seat, looking back at Gwen.

"Are you certain you don't want to sit here?"

The young girl shook her head, a hesitant, wide-eyed half-smile on her pretty face.

Travis said nothing as he opened his door, dropped into the seat behind the steering wheel and turned the key to start the car. Ignoring his passengers, he pulled away from the black courting buggies and the few cars in the field.

Certain now that his behavior had more to do with his *schweschder* than with her, Katie sat back against the soft seat and looked out the window as the countryside sped by them, while she waited for whatever mood he was in to pass.

After several minutes, Gwen leaned forward a bit and spoke quietly. Katie strained to hear her soft voice in the dark vehicle.

"I'm sorry, Gwen. I didn't catch what you said. Could you repeat it, please?"

"I asked you if you sell the lemon cookies you brought tonight at The Sweet Shop."

The question took her by surprise, especially given what she had witnessed earlier between Gwen and her *bruder*.

"*Jah,* we do... or at least I am hoping that we soon will. Lately, I have been working on some new recipes, using lemons as the predominant flavor. Did you try the lemon cookies tonight? And if you had some, what did you think of them?"

"They were awesome! I loved the lemon flavor. Plus the tiny bit of lemon icing was tangy and—well, it was perfect."

"I hope our customers like them as much as you do. I plan to make a batch in the morning for our customers to try."

"What about orange?"

"Orange?"

"Yeah, orange-flavored cookies. Or some other kind of orange-flavored dessert."

Travis made a sound in his throat, but said nothing. After another moment, Katie answered, still curious where Gwen was going with her vague questions.

"The only thing we sell at the bakery

with orange flavoring is a danish."

"Ooh, orange danish sounds wonderful."

Travis let out a little hum of sound, but Gwen went on before he said anything.

"I bet those are good for breakfast; a great way to start the day. I bet you would enjoy starting your day with a visit to the bakery for an orange danish, wouldn't you, Travis?"

Katie was surprised when Travis ignored his *schweschder's* question. Her comment—and her *bruder's* reaction—told Katie there was something more to Gwen's questions than simple curiosity, especially since that was the very danish Travis usually enjoyed for breakfast when he came in to pick up the morning deliveries.

Why, she is trying to match up me with her bruder. Does she know that Travis likes me? Has he said anything to his family to give them the idea that he wants to pursue a courtship... a relationship... with me?

The feelings Katie had been wondering about and worrying over for some time made the questions so much more important now.

Could his feelings for her be more serious than she had imagined?

Would he ask me to leave the plain faith? For sure and for certain, he would not wish to join the church... not for me.

Would I? Could I... leave everything behind?

Travis sat quietly beside her, no sound coming from him as he drove along the gravel lane to her house. There was no hint of his thoughts anywhere in his expression— and Katie dared not ask, though secretly she could not help but wonder what had happened to bring about the questions.

What had Travis said... or done... to give his *schweschder* such an idea?

Katie's parents were sitting on the porch when Katie arrived home. After thanking Travis for the ride home and saying a quick goodbye to Gwen, Katie stepped out of the car and made her way to the steps.

Katie sat down on the top step and looked over at her parents, who were serenely rocking in the porch swing.

"*Gut evening*, Katie. Did you not have a *gut* time? You are home much earlier than we expected you."

"*Nee, Mamm*. I had a *wunderbaar* time. Samuel Yoder was there tonight. He was both nervous and excited to be attending his first singing. Levi was watching over him, while passing out some delicious lemonade made by Mary Zook."

"*Ach*, kinner grow up so quickly." Katie's *mamm* smiled. "It seems only yesterday that young Samuel was eager to start school, and now he is done with schooling and ready to move on with his life. Before we know it, he will be ready to take his instruction and join the church."

Katie's *dat* looked thoughtful.

"*Jah*, and with the Yoders expanding their egg-laying business, young Samuel will be a big help to his family. I am thinking that he will stay pretty busy learning all about how to care for chickens and everything."

After a moment or two of silence, Katie's *mamm* spoke again.

"Katie, your *dat* and I wanted to speak to you about your own plans for the future. We are not trying to push... or rush you... but we were for sure wondering if you had given much thought of when you would be ready to take your instruction and make plans to join the church.

She stopped and looked over at Katie's *dat*. Taking her hand and gently squeezing it, he spoke again.

"*Jah*, there is a baptism class starting up soon... I will admit I was a little concerned last year when you painted the pictures on the bakery window at Christmas, but nothing came of it. You are a *gut* dochder. What your *mamm* and I are trying to say is that we hope you will be praying on this... and will make the right decision."

"*Mamm... Dat...* I know you are only

wanting what is best for me, and I wish I could tell you that I am ready to join the church, but I am just not ready yet.

When her mother started to speak, Katie quickly added, "I have always planned to join the church... I'm just... not ready yet."

Martha Chupp's face showed concern, but she quickly hid it.

"*Dochder*, this is not something you want to rush into. You must be sure that it is what you want... that you are ready... and sure of your decision. Once done, it should never be undone."

"That is it, *Mamm*. I want to be certain that I will never, ever want to leave the church. I want to have no doubts, no worries, no questions. *Ach*, I do not know why I do not feel ready. Perhaps I am too young, after all. I should feel ready... and eager to join the church."

"No, *dochder*." Katie's *dat* broke in. "This is one of the most important decisions you will ever make. You must be sure. Now that we know you are praying on it, we will leave it for now. You should not be feeling any pressure from anyone. When you are ready, you will know for sure."

"Now I think we should go in to sample some of the cookies you brought home today. And you can tell us if the others liked them and if Mrs. Simpkins is going to start selling them." Katie's *mamm* took a deep breath before continuing.

"I have been hearing some strange things from our neighbors about Mrs. Simpkins... and Mr. O'Neal. Is everything going well at the bakery?"

Orange Supreme Bliss Bars

Ingredients:

- 1 box orange supreme cake mix
- 3.4 oz instant vanilla pudding mix
- 4 large eggs
- 1 cup sour cream
- ½ cup milk

Glaze:

- 3 cups powdered sugar
- 4 tbsp orange juice

Instructions:

1. Mix ingredients in a large bowl until blended well.

2. Pour into greased pans and bake at 350 for 20 minutes (or until toothpick inserted in middle comes out clean).

3. Cool on wire racks (be sure to put wax paper under wire racks). Cut into bars.

4. Mix the ingredients of the glaze until smooth and glassy.

5. Pour slowly over cake bars, allowing glaze to run over sides of each bar.

6. Let stand until the glaze is set.

7. Store in cool, dry place.

ELEVEN

Katie looked up at the sound of her name and was surprised to see Gwen looking down at her. The last thing she expected to see at the library was one of the Davis children.

Travis must not have said anything about the singing to their mother, or Gwen would most likely not have been allowed to be out and about town.

"Hey Katie. What are you doing here?"

"I am looking for recipes."

The young girl's expression changed—into one full of mystery and intrigue.

"Ooh. For my brother?"

Katie let out a small sigh before answering. "*Nee*, they are for Freida, my *freind* at the bakery."

"Oh." Gwen's expression changed then—to one of something more than simple disappointment.

I must tread carefully here.

After Gwen had insisted that Travis drive Katie home the night of the singing, and that Katie sit up front with him, it had not taken long for Katie to realize that Gwen was entertaining—perhaps even encouraging—romantic ideas about how Travis felt about her.

Katie, on the other hand, was trying to convince herself that his feelings—and hers—stopped at friendship.

She was fairly certain Travis had done nothing to encourage his little schweschder's ideas, but Gwen was obviously on a mission.

"What brings you to the library today, Gwen?"

"I'm just looking for some new books to read."

Ah, so those books in the front room of their house must be hers. Katie remembered seeing the many shelves filled to bursting with books on her visits to the Davis house.

Since the remainder of the family gathered in the den at the back of the house, she had wondered if the bookcases that were simply overflowing might have actually belonged to their *dat,* especially since she had never seen any of them with a book in their hands or setting beside them—as though they'd just put it down.

"What type of books do you like to read?"

The girl's eyes lit up at the question. "I like to read almost anything. Mysteries, science fiction, fantasy... romance..."

Katie noticed how her voice lowered as she said the last two words, as if she was expecting a reprimand.

"I suppose I am mighty boring by comparison. I mostly like to read cookbooks."

Gwen's head came up in obvious surprise. "But you're such a wonderful baker. Why would you need to read cookbooks?"

"Ah," She held up a finger for emphasis. "Perhaps that is because I read so many cookbooks. Reading about how others put together new recipes helps me to make fewer mistakes when I am creating my own recipes."

"I had not thought of that."

"Anything I bake... or read about... helps me to learn how to create new recipes to tempt and delight those who try them." Katie bit her lip, trying to think of a *gut* example to give her young *freind*.

"If you think about it, it is much like math. First, you learn to add and subtract, making multiplication and division much easier to learn and understand. With baking —or cooking—you start out with basic recipes, then add different ingredients, making the food much more interesting and tasty."

"I'm pretty good at math. I haven't had much of a chance to cook much, but I'm learning. Can you teach me how to make a cake?"

"*Jah*, I can. Last week I made a special cake for the Mayor and his wife; it was three layers, with orange and lemon flavoring in the cake—and in the frosting. The Mayor himself stopped by the bakery to tell Mrs. Simpkins how much their guests enjoyed it."

"Oh, wow! I bet you were pretty excited and proud of what you had created."

"Plain people do not seek *hochmut*—pride. It would not be pleasing to *Gott*."

"Honestly, I don't know if I would want to be Amish... you guys have too many rules."

"*Jah*, that is what most *Englischers* believe, but we believe it makes life easier. When you have no rules, how do you decide what is the right thing to do?"

"Well, most people just do whatever they want to do."

"*Jah*, but sometimes that makes more trouble for everyone. Are you not happier when you follow the rules your *mamm* tells you to follow?"

"I guess so." She looked down, a telltale pink stain spreading across her cheeks and neck.

Clearly she was thinking of the rules she had disobeyed the night of the singing.

After a moment, Gwen looked back up at Katie. The blush was fading and a look of mischief was back in the young *maedel's* eyes.

"Even if I don't want to be Amish, I really like the Amish people I have met. I don't know what we would have done last year if so many people hadn't brought us food and other supplies. And they helped in other ways, too."

Gwen looked up at the big clock on the wall. "Speaking of rules, I have to get home. I don't want to be late and worry my mom. I'll see ya later."

And before Katie could say anything, Gwen was rushing out of the library.

Katie walked back to work, wondering how she might help Gwen. It would be difficult for her at home with four *bruders* and no *schweschders*.

Katie had two younger *schweschders*, but she was blessed with many *freinden* her own age that she could talk to and confide in. She almost laughed out loud when Freida came running out to meet her on the sidewalk.

"Katie, I am glad you returned early from lunch. Mrs. Simpkins asked me to watch out for you. She wants to talk to both of us right away."

"Did she say what she wanted to speak to us about?"

"*Nee*, she just said it was important and for me to watch for you and us to come back to her office as soon as you got back."

"I guess we should go on back now then, *jah*?"

But before they walked into the kitchen, Mrs. Simpkins was coming out of her office to meet them.

"Girls, come on in. This won't take long."

Quickly, the girls made their way to the office.

"Please have a seat. I appreciate

whatever is said in this office to stay just between us."

"Have we done something wrong?" Freida was quick to ask.

Thankfully, she stopped to give her boss time to answer her.

"No, dear. I only wanted to speak to both of you together. I know you probably have questions concerning what's been going on lately, but I would rather not go into all of that right now." She paused for a moment to let her words sink in, then continued.

"I have asked Mr. O'Neal to stop coming by the bakery for awhile. Please trust me when I say that for now, this is how it must be. However, I feel dreadful about my actions —and behavior—during the past few weeks and want to apologize again for being angry, bad-tempered, and generally rude at times. It means everything to me that you girls have stuck by me even while I was cranky and difficult to be around."

Katie spoke up immediately. "Mrs. Simpkins, we love working here. Please do not worry about anything. We just want you to be happy."

"And I feel the same about you as well, both of you. Why, I think of you two as my own, dear girls. I don't know what I'd do without you. I wish I could take you both with me on the cruise, but I don't suppose it would be a good idea to close the bakery for almost a month."

Freida nearly jumped out of her seat.

"Really? You would take us with you? On a big ship out on the ocean for a whole week?"

"Freida, stop. She can't, even if she

wants to. We have to keep the bakery open and running." Katie interrupted her over-zealous *freind*.

Mrs. Simpkins looked a bit embarrassed.

"Oh my dear, yes, I would love to take you with me, but it's just not possible this time. Perhaps there will be another time when it will be possible. Or perhaps when you marry, I can send you and your husband on a cruise."

While Freida peppered Mrs. Simpkins with questions about her upcoming cruise and the idea of a honeymoon cruise, Katie sat quietly, thinking about what her dear, sweet boss had said.

What is it that she is hiding? What could possibly be going on that it has her changing everything about her normal behavior... How serious must it be that she cannot explain?

No matter how Katie thought about it all, there was no answer that made sense. She would simply have to wait for Mrs. Simpkins to decide if and when she could share more about what was going on with her.

——TWELVE——

Freida was waiting when Katie walked up to the door of The Sweet Shop, still humming a little to herself.

"Well, it is about time. What has kept you this morning, Katie Chupp?"

The irritation in her *freind's* voice did not affect Katie's mood one bit. She nearly sang out her "Good morning" as she unlocked the door and walked in, Freida close on her heels.

"It was a *wunderbaar gut* walk today. The sky is clear. The birds are singing. The trees are blooming. Everything is simply beautiful. Monday is Memorial Day. And there is another singing tonight *Gott* is *gut*." At which point, she turned to smile at her *freind*.

Freida was not smiling back. Instead, she turned away and walked behind the counter, although there were no customers since the bakery was not yet open.

"What is wrong? Why are you not in a better mood? You will get to spend time with your sweetheart tonight and you will have a very special cookie to bring him—a cookie you helped to create, if I may remind you."

"I don't know, Katie."

Katie waited for her usually chatty *freind* to say something else, but Freida only stood there on the other side of the counter, silent and frowning.

"*Was iss letz,* Freida? What don't you know?"

"I don't know if I want to join the church or not! I am being silly, I guess. Only... I really want to go on a cruise with Mrs. Simpkins. I want to get out and see the world!"

"Well, but you can "see the world" without leaving the church."

"*Nee*, I cannot. Thomas came by for me last night. He wants us to marry in November. If I agree, I will never get to see the world."

"But you have been wanting to court—wait, Thomas? I thought it was Timothy you were wanting to court. Thomas is so serious all the time. Are you for sure it is Thomas you want?"

"*Jah*, it is Thomas. You can see why he would not be wanting to do things in the world. Why, he has already joined the church."

"If you truly care for Thomas, you should be willing to put aside your own desires. Are you sure you care for him—enough to make a future with him? And if you do not... wait, what did you tell him last night?"

"He did not really give me time to answer him. After I got in his courting buggy and we started down the road, he started talking about his family getting hundreds of chickens, then he said something about building a house and that's when he told me he wanted us to marry in November."

"Well, but why did you not say anything? You never have any trouble talking. Why did you not speak up?"

"Because he kissed me!"

"He—he kissed you?"

"*Jah*."

"But, Freida—"

"I am trying to tell you..." Tears were running down Freida's face now, but Katie had no idea if they were tears of joy or tears of sorrow.

Not knowing what else to do, Katie quickly walked around the counter, where she hugged Freida, patting her back in an effort to calm her.

"Katie, it was the most *wunderbaar* kiss I have ever had!"

Katie's question shot out before she could squelch it. "How many kisses have you had?"

Freida's face turned a warm shade of pink. "Only the one... well, we kissed several times before Thomas took me home, but that was my first time kissing."

"And you never said anything about marrying him—or not?"

"*Nee*, after that first kiss, my brain shut off. Katie, I want to marry him... I am *in lieb* with him. But now you can see why I am upset."

"*Jah*, I can. You are i*n lieb* with Thomas, but you still want to leave our community—to go out into the *Englisch* world."

"*Jah*... *Nee*, I just want to see some things in the world, like what it is like being on a big ship out on the ocean."

"Freida, did you feel this way before Mrs. Simpkins told us she was going on a cruise?"

"*Nee*, not really. I mean, I thought about

seeing places and doing things, but mostly I just wanted Thomas to court me."

"Then why are you upset?"

"I do not know. My brain is still addled by everything that happened last night. I should be *froh*. When Thomas was kissing me, it felt so *wunderbaar*; there was nothing else. But this morning, all I could think of was that maybe I will not make him *froh*. Do you think I could make him *froh*?"

"I think you already do. Even more important, I think he makes you *froh*. But Freida, you should not keep your feelings from him. Tell him how you are feeling— about seeing the world. Then tell him Mrs. Simpkins is going to send you both on a cruise after you marry. Ask him if this is something he would like to do... if it is, there is no problem. You can marry—and see the world, too."

"Katie, you think of everything! I will ask him when he comes for me tonight."

"But Freida, there is one important thing you must do..."

"What is that?"

"You must ask him before he kisses you... and makes you forget everything but his kisses."

Freida giggled. "*Jah*, that is a gut idea."

Grabbing Katie in a hug, Freida swung them around. "*Ach*, I cannot wait until tonight!"

Heading for the kitchen, Katie wondered if Freida was more excited thinking about telling Thomas about the cruise... or thinking of his kisses.

Like any other day, Katie pulled out the ingredients to make nine-grain bread. It was a good thing she was following her normal routine, as her mind was on her conversation with Freida.

Thinking about how Freida went on about how *wunderbaar* it felt kissing Thomas, Katie found herself wondering what it would be like to kiss Travis...

What am I doing? I should not be thinking about kissing—especially about kissing Travis.

Knowing what she should and should not be thinking about did not stop Katie's thoughts.

What if Freida is right? What if we are meant to be together? What if Travis has the same feelings for me? What would I do if he kissed me? Unfortunately, Katie seemed unable to stop herself from thinking about what it might feel like to be kissed—for the very first time—by Travis Davis...

When the young man himself walked into the kitchen a minute later, Katie felt her cheeks flush.

"Hiya, Katie-girl. Penny for your thoughts."

Her cheeks stained a deep pink, Katie was unable to answer him. More embarrassed than she could remember being, Katie fled to Mrs. Simpkin's office and closed the door behind her.

Thankfully the office was empty, so Katie didn't have to worry about explaining her presence to her employer.

A moment later, Katie heard Travis placing boxes on the cart, then rolling it outside. After the door closed again, she heard the sound of another door shutting and, a moment later the sound of the bakery's delivery van.

Knowing she had baking to do and orders to fill, Katie slipped back into the kitchen.

Dear Gott, please take control of this. Please help... I cannot entertain thoughts of courting an Englischer—I cannot. I do not want to leave my family to marry someone outside.

Katie felt better and quickly hurried back to her nine-grain bread.

I know better than to think such thoughts. I just got wrapped up in Freida's news. In another minute, my thoughts would have been on something else.

Oh no! What will Travis think of me— running away from him like I did. Now I will have to apologize for my rude behavior.

Determined to keep her mind on her work, Katie set out to make up for the lost time, working even faster than she normally did.

When Freida came into the kitchen a few minutes later, Katie was placing the dough into individual loaf pans. After covering the pans with a clean cloth, she moved back to the shelves to gather ingredients for peanut butter cookies.

Before Freida had a chance to speak, the back door opened again. This time it was Mrs. Simpkins who came into the kitchen.

"*Gudemariye*, Mrs. Simpkins. How are you doing this morning? Is this not a *wunderbaar* day?"

"Good morning, Freida. I am well, thank you. Good morning, Katie."

"*Gudemariye*, Mrs. Simpkins." Katie replied, but kept her eyes on her work. Without further comment, Mrs. Simpkins went straight to her office and Freida headed back to the front room.

"Katie?"

Katie looked up an hour later when her boss spoke to her.

"Yes, Mrs. Simpkins."

"You have been very quiet this morning. I wanted to make certain you were not upset with me for my recent behavior. Are you all right?"

"Oh no, everything is fine. I just got a bit of a slow start this morning and my mind has been on catching up."

"All right, if you are sure."

Turning to head back to her office, Amelia stopped at the doorway and spoke again. "If there is something bothering you, my door is always open to you."

Katie said nothing, so Amelia went into her office and closed the door.

EPILOGUE

Memorial Day began with beautiful blue skies, soft fluffy clouds, and a warm breeze blowing through the town square.

Everyone was there. Katie had ridden to town with her family, bringing her Triple Lemon Cookies, Lemon Surprise Cupcakes, and Orange Supreme Bliss Bars. Only her *mamm* knew that hidden away in the back of their buggy was a box full of cookies and cupcakes for the Davis family... as well as the Orange Supreme Bliss Bars that Katie had discovered were a special favorite of the young man who still had her feeling a bit flustered.

As per their unusual arrangement, Mr. O'Neal was keeping his distance from Mrs. Simpkins, and his nephew was conspicuously absent.

Katie put several cookies and an orange bliss bar on a plate and meandered over to him.

"*Gudemariye*, Mr. O'Neal. I have brought you several treats to enjoy." As she spoke, she glanced around, looking for her boss.

"Thank you, Katie-girl. What a fine, young *lass* you are to be thinkin' of me." With a quick wink to Katie, Andrew continued. "Now don't ya worry none about me. I have faith that everything will work out in the end. Milly is a stubborn woman, but she can't hold a candle to me. No sir, I can wait around as long as I have to—until she comes to her senses."

Katie could not help but smile at the cheerful determination she heard in Mr. O'Neal's words.

Hearing a scrambling sound, Katie looked away, searching for the source of the odd noise. She noticed a cage on the ground. "What is that?"

"I bet you heard about the rodents in my cafe last week... it turns out that Sean bought a couple of ferrets, but they got loose. When Ada Mueller saw them, she thought they were rats—and she was happy to spread the word."

"Ferrets? I have never heard of them before. Do they make pets?"

"Ya, they make great pets, but since they caused an impromptu visit from the health department, Sean's agreed to sell them. That's why I have them here... so people can see how harmless they are."

"Is that when the police came to your cafe?"

Andrew chuckled out loud. "Is that what people are saying? I get policemen in and out all day... they love my food! Don't tell me... Ada the busybody is spreading rumors again."

"Katie!"

Katie turned to see Freida heading in her direction. Saying goodbye to Mr. O'Neal, she walked back to meet her.

"Katie, Thomas came by again on Saturday night. I did just what you suggested; well, not really. Right after we started out, he kissed me and I forgot all about asking him about the cruise... until later. But it all worked out anyway."

"Tell me what happened. Did he ask you to marry him in November; he needs to ask you."

"Oh *jah*, he stopped the buggy, took my hands in his, and after clearing his throat a time or two, asked me all proper like. Then he asked me if I had any idea of where I would like to go on our honeymoon. That was when I finally mentioned the cruise... and he loved the idea!"

"He did? He really did? That is *wunderbaar*!"

"*Jah*, he even said he had dreamed about taking his *frau* on a cruise some day. With Mrs. Simpkins' offer, we can go right after we marry. I cannot wait until November!"

Freida hugged her *freind*, then laughed.

"Now we need to get you married. Then our *kinner* will be best *freinden*, too."

Katie laughed before saying, "Maybe I should give serious thought to joining the church with you."

"*Jah,* and we will find you a nice man to court in no time." Freida wrapped an arm around Katie's, pulling her toward the festivities.

Smiling, Katie looked around at her family and *freinden*. Everyone was having a *gut* time.

It was time to join them.

Dear Gott, danki for working things out for Freida and Thomas. Bless their marriage... and help me to find the one you have waiting for me.

Katie's Lemon Tarts

Pastry Ingredients:

      1½ cups flour

      1 tbsp sugar

      ¼ tsp salt

      ½ cup butter, chilled

      ¼ cup ice water

Lemon Filling Ingredients:

      3 egg yolks

      1 cup sugar

      6 tbsp cornstarch

      2 cups water

      ½ cup lemon juice

      ¼ tsp salt

      3 tbsp butter

      2 tsp lemon peel, grated

LEMON TART MYSTERY

Instructions:

1. Mix together flour, sugar and salt.

2. Add butter, using a pastry blender or fork (do not over blend).

3. Sprinkle water on the flour mixture, a tbsp at a time, gently mixing with fork until all dough holds together.

4. Form into ball. Let stand several minutes.

5. Roll out dough onto lightly floured surface until thin.

6. Cut in 5" circles (makes 8 tart shells). Fit over inverted custard cups.

7. Pinch together at 4 corners. Prick with fork.

8. Bake at 375(F) 10-12 minutes.

9. Mix sugar and cornstarch in saucepan over low heat. Stir in water.

10. In small bowl, mix lemon juice and egg yolks together. Beat with fork until well

blended. Add to sugar mixture.

11. Stir in salt. Cook over medium heat, stirring constantly, until thick.

12. Continue to cook for 2-3 minutes. Remove from heat.

13. Add butter and grated lemon peel. Stir to blend.

14. Cool for one hour, then spoon onto cooled tart shells.

15. Top with fresh blueberries

Let us therefore come boldly unto the throne of grace, that we may obtain mercy, and find grace to help in time of need.

Hebrews 4:16

RECIPE INDEX

Page   Recipe

51   Lemon Surprise Cupcakes
103   Katie's Triple Lemon Cookies
128   Singing Night Lemonade
155   Orange Supreme Bliss Bars
192   Katie's Lemon Tarts

TURN THE PAGE

FOR EXCLUSIVE

BONUS CONTENT

DISCUSSION QUESTIONS

WARNING : SPOILERS AHEAD!

1) Freida and Katie have been friends all their lives. How important are friendships? Do you have friends that you've known for many years?

2) Freida apologizes to Katie... then Mrs. Simpkins apologizes to both girls. Do you extend apologies when needed? Do you find it difficult to apologize?

3) Mrs. Simpkins is no longer seeing Mr. O'Neal. Relationships are hard to maintain. What is the longest relationship you have had?

4) The Yoders are getting ready to care for more than a hundred chickens, plus gathering the eggs and preparing them to sell to customers. There are lots of rules when selling products to the public. Do you think it's worth the trouble? Do you think mass producing food is a viable option?

5) In Abbott Creek, the Amish families begin thinking about marriage and family much sooner than the English families. Do you think it is a good idea to make

plans when you're in your teens? Or should people wait until they're older?

6) Do you believe marriage is meant to be for a lifetime? Are there reasons that divorce should be allowed? How do you think divorce affects the children in a marriage? How can problems be overcome and the marriage saved?

7) Katie eventually decides to join the church and marry someone who belongs to the church. Freida thought she should give Travis a chance... What do you think? Would you change your faith for someone else? Should you?

AUTHOR INTERVIEW

Q: What was your inspiration for writing Lemon Tart Mystery?

A: I believe people are tempted by choices that may or may not hurt their walk with God. Maybe Katie will stay with her church, or maybe she will leave and marry an Englischer... either choice could hurt her.

I also wanted the chance to show how people can say and do things to hurt or offend others. When this happens, they need to be sorry—and seek forgiveness. When someone apologizes, we should be ready to forgive.

Q: What do you hope your readers will take away from reading Lemon Tart Mystery—or others in the series?

A: That faith, family, and forgiveness aren't just words, but should be practiced in our daily lives.

Q: Will there be more books in the Amish Sweet Shop Mystery series?

A: Oh, yes. I'm working on book four now, titled

Pumpkin Pie Mystery, which I hope will be released later this year.

Q: What does your writing space look like?
A: My writing space is a beautiful desk, left to me by my sister. But, most of the time, I'm either sitting at the dining room table, or sitting on the couch, with my laptop. Honestly, I can write most anywhere.

Q: What is your favorite Bible verse and why?
A: I have many favorites—too many to list all of them, but I'm happy to share one with you today!
"Trust in the Lord with all thine heart; and lean not unto thine own understanding. In all thy ways acknowledge him, and he shall direct thy paths."
~Proverbs 3:5-6

Q: Do you have a favorite scene in your newest release?
A: Honestly, my favorite scene is when Freida is teasing Katie about being in love with Travis. It's the perfect "friend" scene. And when Katie insists that it can't work, is she trying to convince Freida? Or herself?

Q: Where can readers connect with you?

A: Here are the links for each site:

NEWSLETTER SIGN UP: http://eepurl.com/bPdjGn
WEBSITE: https://naomimillerauthor.com
FACEBOOK: www.facebook.com/NaomiMillerAuthor
TWITTER: https://twitter.com/AuthorNaomi
INSTAGRAM: https://twitter.com/AuthorNaomi
PINTEREST: http://www.pinterest.com/authornaomi
GOODREADS: http://bit.ly/1VMIegX
INDIEBOUND: http://bit.ly/1PsB9MR
FICTION FINDER: http://bit.ly/1UOlI5P

I would also like to take a moment here to point out that there are several mentions of Katie's cousin—who lives in upstate New York. This was done with permission from my fellow author Rachel L. Miller. Yes, it is the same Leah Fisher from her upcoming release: *A Mother for Leah*.

ACKNOWLEDGMENTS

To God be the glory! HE is THE AUTHOR of my life! God gives me the inspiration for each and every book... books of family, faith, forgiveness, and grace...

When God placed it on my heart to write a light-hearted mystery series, I'm glad I obeyed.

Thanks to my daughter Rachel, who not only designs my covers, memes, posters (well, you get the picture), but is also an amazing author and inspirational speaker.

Rachel, I couldn't have done it without you!

A big thank you goes out to Pam, my dear friend and founder of S&G Publishing. If not for Pam, I might never have been published!

Last, but by no means least, thank you to my awesome readers, who do so much to encourage me and continue make this series a huge success!

ABOUT THE AUTHOR

Naomi Miller mixes up a batch of intrigue, sprinkled with Amish, Mennonite, and English characters, adding a pinch of mystery—and a dash of romance!

Naomi works full time as an author, blogger and inspirational speaker. She is a member of the American Christian Fiction Writers (ACFW) organization.

When she's not working diligently to finish the next novel in her Sweet Shop Mystery series, Naomi tries to make time for attending workshops, writing conferences and other author events. Whenever time permits, Naomi can be found in one of two favorite places—the beach and the mountains.

Naomi's day is spent focusing on her writing, editing, and blogging about her experiences. Naomi loves traveling with her family, singing inspirational/gospel music, taking a daily walk, and witnessing to others of the amazing grace of Jesus Christ.

DON'T MISS THE NEXT BOOK IN THIS SERIES
COMING THIS YEAR!

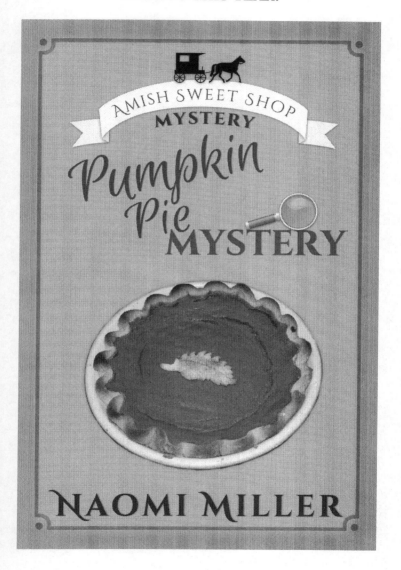

AMISH SWEET SHOP

MYSTERY

Pumpkin Pie
MYSTERY

NAOMI MILLER

ABOUT THE PUBLISHER

Christian Publishing for HIS GLORY

S&G Publishing offers books with messages that honor Jesus Christ to the world! S&G works with Christian authors to bring you the best in "inspirational" fiction and non-fiction.

S&G is proud to publish a variety of Christian fiction genres:

inspirational romance

young reader

young adult

speculative

historical

suspense

Check out our website at

sgpublish.com

MORE FROM

S&G PUBLISHING

COMING SOON

A
Mother
for
Leah

"Sweet, compelling, and filled with a charming cast of
characters who will resonate with readers of all ages."
~ Suzanne Woods Fisher, bestselling author of *The Quieting*

WINDY GAP WISHES
BOOK ONE

Rachel L Miller

Junior author series

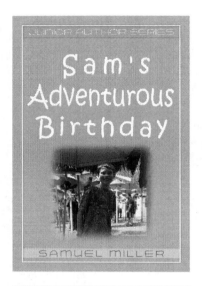

Author encouragement series

NEW FROM JC MORROWS

Made in the USA
Middletown, DE
23 August 2017